Bat-em-in Benjie

By
Chanie
Friedman

Illustrated by
Norman Nodel

The bases were loaded, the tension was great
When "Bat-'em-in" Benjie stepped up to the plate.
It was right at the bottom of the very last inning
With Bat-'em-in-Benjie's team three runs from winning.
But a fourth run would really make Benjie's head spin
'Cause he'd break the league record for runs batted in!

Benjie glanced to his left; he glanced to his right
Then he picked up the bat, and with all of his might
He swung! And the ball met the bat with a pop!
It sailed through the air...would that ball ever stop?

The crowd all went wild as they yelled in a roar
"Here is the moment you've been waiting for!
To break the league record, just score this home run
Then, Bat-'em-in Benjie, you'll be number one!"

As fast as the wind, Benjie headed for first

Reached second so quickly he thought he might burst.

To third he just flew, why his shoes left no mark. Then he made a sharp turn... and ran out of the park.

The crowd stopped their screaming, you could hear a pin drop.
The umpire's jaw just dropped open...kerplop!
Then from out of the stands came a voice speaking low,
"Hey, what's going on here? Where did that kid go?"

"Pinch me, I'm dreaming," a second one said.
"Did I see what I saw?" he asked, scratching his head.
"You saw what you saw," the crowd called in reply,
"That kid just ran off and we'd like to know why!
We'd like to know why, and we'd rather not wait!"

Just then Bat-'em-in Benjie strolled back through the gate.

"Hey, Bat-'em-in Benjie, you know what you've done?
You ran the wrong way and just blew your home run!
Did you lose all your senses, or just lose your way?
Well, Bat-em-in Benjie, what have you to say?"

"I can see you're confused, so I'll try to explain
Why I let a home run just slip right down the drain."
Then Bat-'em-in Benjie sat down on the mound
And called to the crowd, "Come on, gather round.
I'll be glad to relate the events that took place.
At precisely the moment I rounded third base.

As I was running with wings on my feet
It happened, by chance, that I glanced 'cross the street
Where I saw Rabbi Brown coming out of a store
With his arms full of packages, seven or more!
And I thought, in a flash, ' I should go lend a hand,'
So I went...and I hoped you would all understand."

"Well, we do understand that you did a good deed
When you rushed off to help out a person in need.
But, Bat-'em-in Benjie, you were close to home plate...
It's great to do mitzvos—BUT COULDN'T IT WAIT?"

"YES, COULDN'T IT WAIT?" the crowd's cry now grew greater,
"A MITZVAH'S A MITZVAH STILL, THREE SECONDS LATER!"

Now, Bat-'em-in Benjie let out a great sigh.
"I, too, once believed I could let time slip by.
Before doing a mitzvah I knew I should do
I'd think and rethink till I thought the thing through.
And when all of my thinking was over, at last
I'd find that the time for the mitzvah had passed."

"Please tell us about it," the crowd drew in near.
We're really quite anxiously waiting to hear
How you came to discover what you seem to now know
When a good deed needs doing, just get up and go."

"Well, it's quite a long story, but I'm happy to tell
How I learned this great lesson I now know so well."

"You remember last summer when Eli Levine
Went out to the country to visit Sol Green?
One day they picked flowers and it was no joke
When Eli picked something that's called Poison Oak."

"Oy vay, I remember," said Mrs. Levine.
(She'd come to the ball park to root for her team.)
"He returned on the very first bus he could catch,
Then he lay on his bed all day long and he scratched.
He only stopped scratching when friends came to call.
But Bat-'em-in Benjie did not come at all."

"I did not come at all though I knew and know still
It's a mitzvah to visit a friend who is ill.
But instead of just going, what did I do?
I thought and rethought till I thought the thing through."

"On Monday I thought:
What if I get there and knock on the door.
And Eli is sleeping, I'll wake him mid-snore.
He'll jump out of bed and while still in a daze
He'll stumble and knock down his mother's good vase.
Then Mrs. Levine will be awfully upset
Oh my, what a talking-to Eli will get.
He'll lose his allowance for a week, maybe more
And all this because I just knocked on his door.

Why this really might happen, the chances are good
I'm not saying it will, I'm just saying it could."

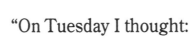

"On Tuesday I thought:
I'm off to see Eli, I'll leave right away
We'll have a fine visit, it's such a nice day
We'll sit in the yard and enjoy the cool breeze
I only hope Eli won't catch a cold and sneeze
He'll sneeze in the daytime, he'll sneeze through the night
And all the between time, he'll scratch. What a sight!
All that sneezing and scratching... scratch, sneeze,
scratch...ah choo.
Sneeze first? Or scratch first? Oh, what will he do?

This can really occur, I can see how it would.
There's no way to be certain, but chances are good."

"On Wednesday I thought:
I'm visiting Eli, this time there's no doubt.
I can't understand what the fuss was about.
I'll just march to his house and say 'Hi! How are you?'
Then his mother will offer a cookie or two.
And I'll certainly eat one, her cookies are great!
In fact, I'll eat two...or seven...or eight
Or twenty...or forty, what if I can't stop?
I'll just keep it up till I fill to the top.
And oh, what a terrible guest I will make
As I moan and I groan from a great belly ache.

Why the chances are good this could really take place
I can not say for sure, but it might be the case."

"Now, on Thursday I thought:
Well, three days have passed, and I've got a plan
To visit with Eli as soon as I can.
But first I will call to make sure he's awake
And ask him to put away things that can break.
There's nothing to fear from a chill in the air
If I just bring a sweater for Eli to wear.
To offers of cookies I'll say, ' Thank you, no! '

There, I've thought it all through, so tomorrow...I go!"

Now, Bat-'em-in Benjie stood up on the mound
And for several long seconds did not make a sound.
He looked round at the crowd and he asked, speaking low,
"Can you guess what occurred when I did, at last, go?"

"No need to guess," spoke up Mrs. Levine.
"Let's not forget I was there at the scene.
Bat-'em-in Benjie called Friday, that's true.
First, he explained how he'd thought the thing through.
And then he announced he was coming at last.
But for doing this mitzvah, the moment had passed.
You see, Eli was better... that's what I mean...

He'd gone back to the country to visit Sol Green."

Then Bat-'em-in Benjie said, "That was the day
I learned that a mitzvah's best done right away.
Now nothing can stop me from getting one done
No, not even the chance to score a home run!"

Now the crowd buzzed aloud with the story they'd heard
But it was the umpire who had the last word:
"Bat-'em-in Benjie may not be a name
That ever goes down in the Sports Hall of Fame
But for doing his mitzvos with super-quick speed
Bat-'em-in Benjie's a hero, indeed."

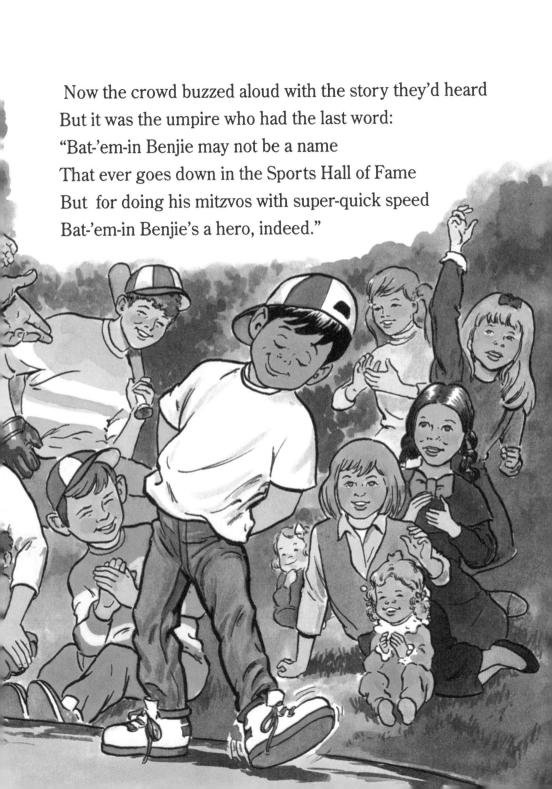

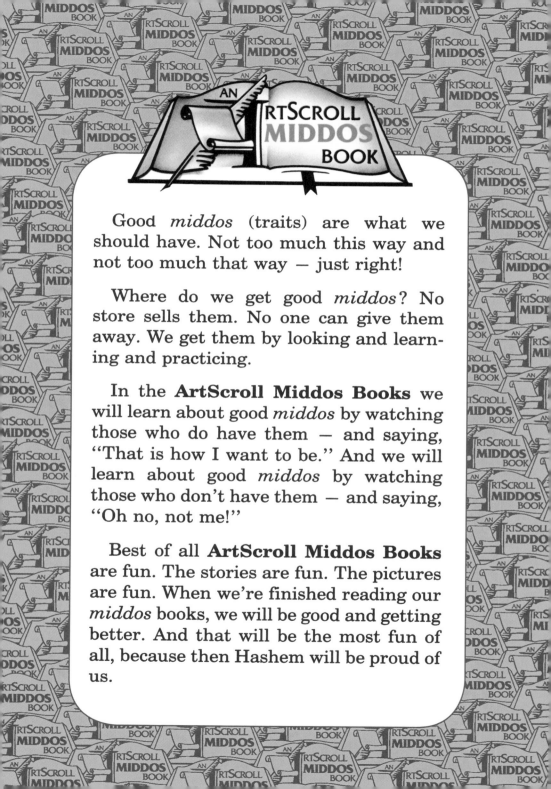

Good *middos* (traits) are what we should have. Not too much this way and not too much that way — just right!

Where do we get good *middos*? No store sells them. No one can give them away. We get them by looking and learning and practicing.

In the **ArtScroll Middos Books** we will learn about good *middos* by watching those who do have them — and saying, "That is how I want to be." And we will learn about good *middos* by watching those who don't have them — and saying, "Oh no, not me!"

Best of all **ArtScroll Middos Books** are fun. The stories are fun. The pictures are fun. When we're finished reading our *middos* books, we will be good and getting better. And that will be the most fun of all, because then Hashem will be proud of us.